Red was not big.
His home was at the
top of an oak.
His mom fed him.

"I like to eat," said Red.
His mom had to get him
a lot to eat.

2

"I am big," said Red.
"I can take a hike."

Red came to a leaf.
Red and the leaf made
a dive.

Red hit his beak on
the road.
Red was sad and did
not see his mom.

Red ran.
Red came to a dog.

Red sat on his tail.
"Beat it," said the dog.

Red ran on.
"That dog was mean,"
said Red.

Red came to a hose.
Red sat on the hose.

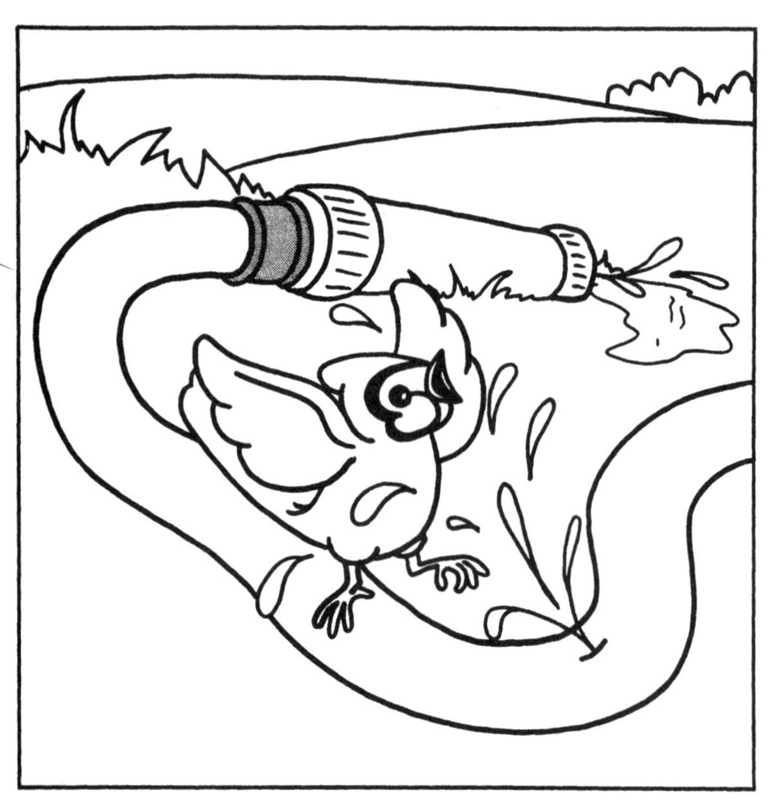

The hose had a leak
in it.
Red got wet.

"That hose was mean,"
said Red.
Red ran on.

Red came to Bob
and Rob.
It was time to eat
and Red did not see
his mom.

"Red is weak and has
to eat," said Rob.
"I can lead him home."

Rob got Red up on a
vine.

Rob got Red home to
his mom.
Mom fed Red his meal.

"Rob is not mean," said
Red to his mom.
"Rob is a real pal."